A MOUSY MESS

by **Laura Driscoll** • Illustrated by **Deborah Melmon**

THE KANE PRESS / NEW YORK

With thanks to the three J's: Joanne, Judy, and Juliana—L.D.

Acknowledgments: We wish to thank the following people for their helpful advice and review of the material contained in this book: Susan Longo, Early Childhood and Elementary School Teacher, Mamaroneck, NY; and Rebeka Eston Salemi, Kindergarten Teacher, Lincoln School, Lincoln, MA.

Special thanks to Susan Longo for providing the Fun Activities in the back of this book.

Library of Congress Cataloging-in-Publication Data

Driscoll, Laura.
A mousy mess / by Laura Driscoll ; illustrated by Deborah Melmon.
pages cm. — (Mouse math)
Summary: Albert the mouse and his big sister, Wanda, have fun in the playroom of the People House where they live, then must quickly sort and return everything to its proper place before the people return.
ISBN 978-1-57565-646-5 (library reinforced binding : alk. paper) — ISBN 978-1-57565-647-2 (pbk. : alk. paper)
[1. Mice—Fiction. 2. Set theory—Fiction. 3. Toys—Fiction. 4. Brothers and sisters—Fiction.] I. Melmon, Deborah, illustrator. II. Title.
PZ7.D79Mou 2014
[E]—dc23
2013038562

eISBN: 978-1-57565-648-9

1 3 5 7 9 10 8 6 4 2

First published in the United States of America in 2014 by Kane Press, Inc.
Printed in the United States of America

Book Design: Edward Miller

Mouse Math is a registered trademark of Kane Press, Inc.

Visit us online at **www.kanepress.com**

Like us on Facebook
facebook.com/kanepress

Follow us on Twitter
@KanePress

Dear Parent/Educator,

"I can't do math." Every child (or grownup!) who says these words has at some point along the way felt intimidated by math. For young children who are just being introduced to the subject, we wanted to create a world in which math was not simply numbers on a page, but a part of life—an adventure!

Enter Albert and Wanda, two little mice who live in the walls of a People House. Children will be swept along with this irrepressible duo and their merry band of friends as they tackle mouse-sized problems and dilemmas (and sometimes *cat-sized* problems and dilemmas!).

Each book in the **MOUSE MATH**® series provides a fresh take on a basic math concept. The mice discover solutions as they, for instance, use position words while teaching a pet snail to do tricks or count the alarmingly large number of friends they've invited over on a rainy day—and, lo and behold, they are doing math!

Math educators who specialize in early childhood learning have applied their expertise to make sure each title is as helpful as possible to young children—and to their parents and teachers. Fun activities at the ends of the books and on our website encourage kids to think and talk about math in ways that will make each concept clear and memorable.

As with our award-winning Math Matters® series, our aim is to captivate children's imaginations by drawing them into the story, and so into the math at the heart of each adventure. It is our hope that kids will want to hear and read the **MOUSE MATH** stories again and again and that, as they grow up, they will approach math with enthusiasm and see it as an invaluable tool for navigating the world they live in.

Sincerely,

Joanne Kane

Joanne E. Kane
Publisher

Albert skipped as his big sister, Wanda,
led the way to the People House playroom.
Their friend Leo was coming with them.

"I can't believe my mom said we can go!"
Albert said.

The playroom was a long way from home. So it was usually off limits. But lately, things had been different. . . .

The People had been away for days.
They had packed suitcases—and even the cat.

Then they had put everything in the car and driven away.

"We don't know when the People will be home," Wanda warned. "So we have to be ready to leave quickly. *And* we must put *everything* back— or they'll know we've been here!"

Albert gulped. What would happen if the People found out they had been in the playroom?

But soon they were there . . . and Albert forgot about worrying. There were too many things to play with!

Leo tried out the marbles first.

Wanda zipped right over to the books.

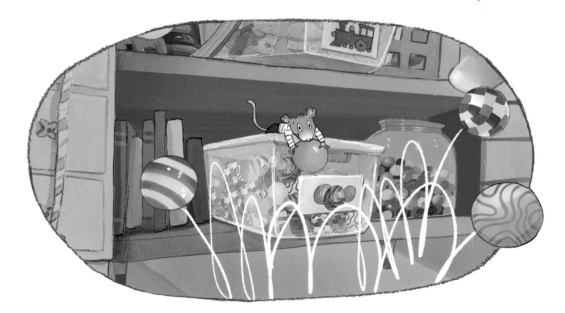

Albert darted from one bin to the next.
"Wow!" he cried, bouncing the balls.

"Wheeee!" he shouted, sliding down a train track.

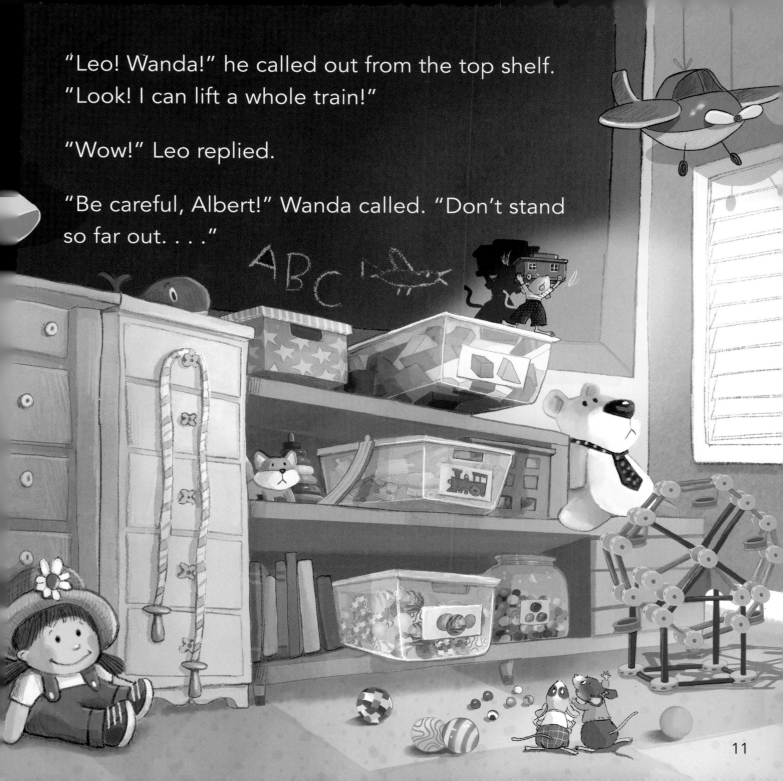

"Leo! Wanda!" he called out from the top shelf. "Look! I can lift a whole train!"

"Wow!" Leo replied.

"Be careful, Albert!" Wanda called. "Don't stand so far out. . . ."

11

It was too late. "Whoaaa!" Albert cried as the bin toppled.

He grabbed onto a shelf, but the bin kept falling, knocking over other bins as it went. **Bonk! Bonk!**

Wanda and Leo dove for cover!

Together, the three mice stared at the mess.
"Uh-oh," Leo said.

"Oh, no!" Albert panicked. They had to get everything
put away, or the People would know they'd been there!

But how?

"I'll get more mice to help," Wanda said. "You start sorting these things so we can put them back in the right bins. Just make piles of toys that are *similar*, or the same in some way."

With that, Wanda scurried off.

"Hmm," said Albert. "Which toys are similar?" He looked at a blue marble and a blue block. "These are the same color—blue. I'll make a blue pile!" He added a blue train car.

Leo picked up a yellow marble and a red ball. "These have a round, roll-y shape," he said. "I'll start a pile of round, roll-y things!"

Albert and Leo zipped around, making piles.
"Small things!"

"Big things!"

"Red things!"

Albert picked up a blue ball and headed for the blue pile.
Then he stopped. Should it go in the round, roll-y pile
instead? Or maybe the big pile?

Soon Wanda returned with a bunch of mouse friends.

"You two have been busy!" she said, looking around at all the piles.

Wanda pointed to the picture label on each bin.
"But we only need *four* piles: one for marbles,
one for blocks, one for balls, and one for trains."

Albert and Leo stared at each other.
They had to sort everything *all over again*?

"You can sort in lots of different ways," said Wanda,
"and you did! You sorted some things by color . . .

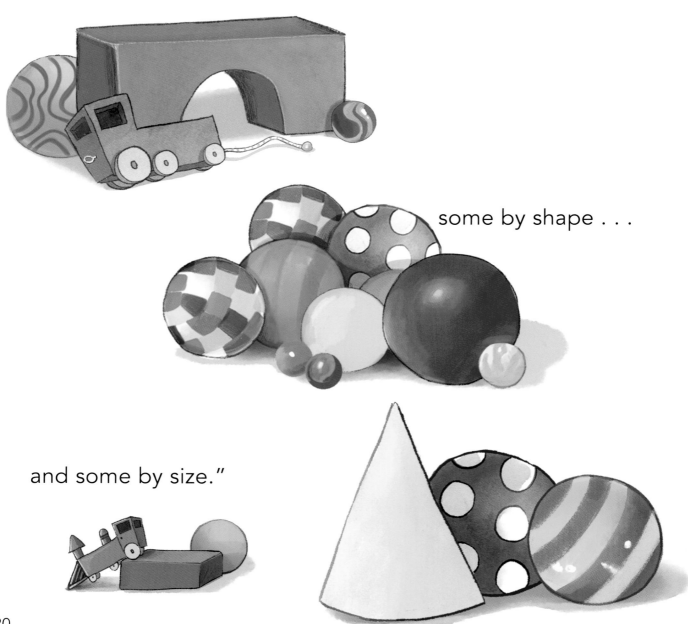

some by shape . . .

and some by size."

"But we need to sort everything by the kind of toy it is," Wanda said. "These are both marbles. So they go in the marble jar."

Wanda explained that all the trains went in the train bin, all the blocks went in the block bin, and all the bouncy balls went in the bouncy ball bin.

Luckily, Albert and Leo had lots of help now.

Before long, there was just one marble left on the floor. "I've got it!" Albert exclaimed. He tucked it under his shirt, then climbed up to put it away all by himself.

But standing on the marble jar, Albert had trouble
getting the marble out from under his shirt.
He tugged and pulled and—

"Whoa!" Albert cried as he fell in.

At that moment, the mice heard the front door open—and voices. "Oh, no!" Wanda said. "The People are back!"

Mice ran for the mouse hole—all except Leo and Wanda, who raced to help Albert.

"Hurry, Albert!" said Wanda. "Grab my paw!"

Albert stretched, but he couldn't quite reach.
The marbles under him kept moving!

Just then, a large furry face appeared in the doorway.
The *CAT!*

"Leo!" Wanda yelled. "Quick—tip the jar!"
They hung off the rim. The jar tipped.
And Albert poured out along with ALL the marbles!

The mice raced toward the hole as marbles rolled
across the floor.

The cat sprang—and hit the marbles. He slipped and slid
while Albert, Wanda, and Leo dove for the mouse hole.

"We made it!" Albert said. "But that was so close. And Wanda, we left a *huge* mess."

Wanda laughed. "Yes," she said. "But lucky for us, the People will never know it's a *mousy* mess!"

A Mousy Mess supports children's understanding of **sorting, attributes, and classifying**, important topics in early math learning. Use the activities below to extend the math topics and to support children's early reading skills.

ENGAGE

▶ Begin by directing children to look at the illustration on the cover. (You may wish to cover up the title so as not to give away the answer.) Encourage children to discuss what they think the story might be about. Record their predictions and refer to them after reading the story.

▶ Show children the title and read it aloud. Ask if they have ever made a mess at home or in school. Encourage children to tell their stories and share how they made the mess and how they cleaned it up. Did they need help? You may hear some very funny stories!

▶ Say: *Now it's time to read the story and find out what happens to Albert!*

LOOK BACK

▶ After reading the story, have children tell the story in their own words. What happens in the beginning of the story? What happens in the middle? What happens at the end?

▶ Ask children to describe how Albert and Leo sort the toys on the floor while Wanda is away gathering friends to help. Do they sort by color, by size, by kind of toy? Have children refer back to the story for help. Begin a list titled "Ways to Sort." List children's suggestions about how Albert and Leo sort the toys.

▶ What does Wanda do when she returns with more mouse friends? How does she want the toys sorted? Why? Add the ways the mice now begin to sort the toys to the "Ways to Sort" list. Reinforce the idea that sorting can be done in many ways.

▶ Ask: *How would you sort the toys in the story?* Have children share their thoughts first with a partner and then with the group. Ask: *Did you discover any new ways to sort the toys?* Add children's responses to the "Ways to Sort" list.

🐭 TRY THIS!

Sorting Fun!

▶ Provide children with plastic containers and tell them to collect 15 things from the room (blocks, crayons, toy money, play food, etc.) to put in their container. (You can vary the number of items. You may also have the children partner up or work in small groups.)

▶ Once children have collected 15 things, tell them to sort the items into different piles. Tell children that they can look at the "Ways to Sort" list for ideas. Have them share the different ways they chose to sort their items.

🐭 THINK!

Let's play **Discover My SORT!** (a sorting and attribute game)

Materials you'll need: attribute blocks, two long lengths of yarn

▶ Gather blocks of different shapes, colors, and sizes. Then tie the ends of one length of yarn together, place it on the floor, and adjust it to form a circle.

▶ Decide how you want children to sort the blocks (for example: blocks that are yellow, or blocks that are small), but do not tell them what you have chosen. Children will discover the attribute by trial and error.

▶ Say: *I've decided how I want you to sort the blocks, but I won't tell you. You'll be able to figure it out by seeing which blocks I let you put inside the circle and which blocks I don't let you put there. I'll say "yes" if the block has the right attribute and belongs in the circle and "no" if it doesn't belong.* Be sure children understand the game.

▶ Have children take turns placing a block in the circle. Confirm whether or not the block belongs in the circle by saying "yes" or "no." Remind children to pay attention to the kinds of blocks you allow in the circle and the kinds you do not. As more children take turns, they should discover the attribute.

▶ **Challenge:** Follow the same rules as above, but use two circles of yarn that overlap, forming an area in the middle. (The yarn should resemble a Venn diagram.) This time, think of two attributes that children will have to discover by recognizing how the blocks in the middle are alike. (For example, if you choose "big" and "yellow" as the attributes, the big, yellow blocks will go in the overlapping middle section; the big blocks that are not yellow will go in the area to the left; the yellow blocks that are not big will go in the area to the right.) Repeat for more sorting fun!

◆ **FOR MORE ACTIVITIES** ◆

visit www.kanepress.com/mouse-math-activities